On j....

she was asked by C.S. Lewis to illustrate his
Narnia books in 1950, and in 1968
she was awarded the prestigious Kate Greenaway
Medal. An honour which places her among the
foremost of children's illustrators.
Pauline Baynes is one of the most original,
versatile and brilliant artists of our time.

THE *Little* CHAIR

RUMER GODDEN

ILLUSTRATED BY
PAULINE BAYNES

Hodder
Children's
Books

a division of Hodder Headline plc

In my house there is a little chair, just twenty inches high, which is older than any of us. It is made of oak so old that the wood has a warm glow, and it has a rush seat; although many children have sat on it, the rush is still the same rush; it has two wooden arm rails, comfortable for three-to five-year-olds.

The little chair was made for my Great-Great-Aunt Emma in 1836, more than a hundred and fifty years ago, and I have known five sets of children in our family who, down the years, have sat on it, listening to stories, "Once upon a time . . ."

Text Copyright © 1996 Rumer Godden
Illustrations Copyright © 1996 Pauline Baynes

First published in Great Britain in 1996
by Hodder Children's Books
This paperback edition first published in 1996
by Hodder Children's Books

The right of Rumer Godden and Pauline Baynes to be identified as the Author and the illustrator of
the Work has been asserted by them in accordance with the Copyright, Designs and Patents Act
1988.

10 9 8 7 6 5 4 3 2 1

A Catalogue record for this book is available from the British Library

ISBN 0 340 64843 0

Printed and bound by Bell and Bain Ltd., Glasgow

Hodder Children's Books
A Division of Hodder Headline plc
338 Euston Road
London NW1 3BH

To all the children who
have sat in it.

Great-Great-Aunt Emma
herself came to see us when my
sister Ruth and I were staying
in our grandmother's house in
London. She arrived in a closed
carriage, painted dark green,
whose coachman and footman
wore tall hats with dark green
cockades to match.

The coachman had a long whip and there was a pair of bay horses, their coats shining. We should dearly have loved to pat them but were not allowed.

Great-Great-Aunt Emma was
very old with a black lace veil
over her beautiful white hair.

She gave us two big jointed dolls
dressed in stiff white satin,
embroidered one in pink for Ruth,
one in blue for me. We called
them Rosebud and Bluebell, but
we were only allowed to play
with them on Sundays, which
meant we never liked them.
Grown-ups do not seem to
understand that if you have a
doll you want her – or him – to
live with you all the time.

We tried to put Rosebud and
Bluebell in the chair but their
dresses would not come off and
were so stiff they could not sit
down.

I don't think the little chair
liked them either.

When our grandmother, Harriet, was a little girl, every evening at five o'clock she was changed and went down to the drawing room.

Winter and summer she wore a muslin dress with a blue sash and blue bows catching up the sleeves to her shoulders, leaving her arms and neck bare, and pantalettes, white cotton drawers long to her ankles and edged with lace.

The only heating in the house came from fires in the rooms, so that the stairs, corridors and hall were icy cold; in winter Harriet's nurse gave her a little white

shawl but she had to take it off in the drawing room. All the same, she sat in the little chair by the fire while her mother read stories to her.

When Harriet grew up she had eight children – it was a wonder the chair did not wear out. The youngest but one was my father, Arthur. Arthur did not do much sitting: he was a naughty little boy and spoiled because he was so good-looking.

The nurseries in that London home were at the top of the house, up three flights of stairs.

One day Arthur was told to take a pudding to his sisters, who were ill in bed. The pudding was a blancmange, rather like a jelly but, as it was made with milk, it was heavier and more splodgy. It shook on its dish as Arthur carried it.

On the top landing he stopped and looked over the banisters: far down below he could see the curving staircase and the black and white marble squares of the hall floor.

He could not stop himself. He turned the dish upside down and dropped the blancmange over the banisters. It fell,

down,

down,

down,

till it landed with a plop, squelch
on the hall floor.

We loved to hear him tell that
story and I am sure the little chair
liked children who were bad as
well as the ones who were good.

Then it came to Ruth and me, Arthur's daughters who were left with Harriet, our grandmother, in the London house while he and our mother were away in India.

At five o'clock we, too, had to
get out of our comfortable skirts
and jerseys and into frocks, not
muslin, I am glad to say, but
brown velvet with a lace collar in
winter, pale blue silk in summer,
and go down to the drawing
room where we were forced to
do hated embroidery and read
to Grandmother Harriet.

Ruth was too big to sit in the
chair so I had it to myself till
six o'clock.

I dreaded six o'clock because being younger – five to Ruth's seven – I was sent up to bed half an hour before her. As I have told, the nurseries were at the top of the house, and on the first floor landing a huge stuffed bear stood on its back legs, its dreadful front paws, with their long claws, hanging down. Father Arthur had shot him in India.

In those days the house did
not have electricity, only gas
lamps that flickered. The bear's
eyes flickered too – they were
glass but I did not know that and
was sure he was alive. I had to
pass him; most nights when I
reached the night nurseries I had
wet my lace-edged knickers and
was punished.

When I grew up I had Jane and Paula. They liked to sit turn by turn in the chair while I told them stories. The stories always began in the same way:

"Once upon a time there were two little girls, one with hair like marmalade, and one with hair like honey."

Grown-ups should never make children show off when they don't want to: the little chair knew that.

Jane and Paula's cousin came to stay with us and, as he was the youngest, he sat in the little chair.

Simon was not only a beautiful
little boy, he was clever and, like
many clever children, he would
pick up words and say them as a
little parrot would, not knowing
what they meant; but he, like
me, loved words and, "Say the
tiny little boy, heyho poem," he
would say to me.

When that I was a tiny little boy,
With a heyho the wind and the rain
A foolish thing was but a toy
For the rain, it raineth every day.

"What does foolish mean?"
Paula, who was a year older,
would have asked, but Simon
just said the lovely words.

We were staying with their grandfather – Arthur of the blancmange pudding – and he was especially proud of Simon. One day he and his wife gave a big lunch party and the children came in, as he liked them to do, to say, "How do you do", and hand round nuts and crisps. He said proudly, "This is my grandson Simon. He is only four but he knows Shakespeare. Simon, tell the ladies and gentlemen the poem you learnt at school."

(Grandfather Arthur didn't know
that I said poems to the children;
he thought poetry belonged to
schools, and Simon and Paula
went to playschool.)

"Say it, Simon."

Simon went pink. "No, thank you," he said.

"Simon!"
"No."

But Grandfather Arthur was stern, "Do as I tell you," and poor Simon began.

"Red, white and blue,
Old man Kangaroo,
Sitting by the dustbin
Busy doing poo."

"But I *did* learn it at school," he sobbed when he was banished, sent out in disgrace.

MARK

EMMA

ELIZABETH

CHARLOTTE

Jane had four children, Mark, Elizabeth, Emma and Charlotte, my grandchildren – Emma was the naughty one. When Emma did not like anything or anyone she did something about it.

Once, when Jane was going to
stay a few days with me, Florence,
their other grandmother, was
coming to look after her and
Charlotte in their country home
– Mark and Elizabeth were away
at boarding school. Florence was
strict and forbade all kinds of
things, which made Emma
angry and unhappy.

FLORENCE

The spare room in their house was upstairs off the landing, down a dark little passage that had three steps, rather dark too. Just before Jane left to catch her train, she went up to the spare room to see if it was ready for Florence . . . and what did she find? On those steep dark steps was a network of strings, strong string stretched from side to side and held firm by tin tacks.

Of course, Jane knew at once who had done it. "Emma, what is this? You did it, didn't you?"

"Oh, yes," said Emma, "it's a Gran-trap", and quite enough to catch their particular gran and trip her up. Florence was a big woman and would have fallen heavily.

"Oh, Emma, you might have hurt her badly."

42

Emma was six, too old to sit in the chair but she went and knelt in front of it, put her elbows on the seat and hid her face in her hands. Presently a tear dropped on the rushes.

❊ *The Family Tree* ❊

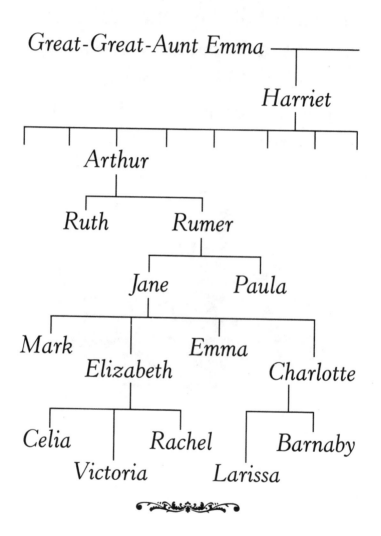

Great-Great-Aunt Emma was my great-great-aunt.

Harriet, her niece, was my grandmother.

Harriet's son, Arthur, was my father.

I am Jane and Paula's mother.

Jane's children are my grandchildren, and now I am great-grandmother to their children:

Celia   8
Victoria   6
Rachel   4
Larissa   3
and Barnaby.

Celia and Victoria have outgrown the little chair; Rachel and Larissa take turns in it;

Barnaby cannot sit in the chair because he can't sit up yet – he is only four months old – but the little chair is holding out its arms and saying,

"Ready."